DANCE OF THE FIRE CAT – A TALE OF GRIMALHAME

ISBN: 978-1-9999523-8-9

Copyright © 2024 Angela Russell. All rights reserved.

Grimalhame Press®

Clowder of Grimalhame®

First Published by AuthorHouse 2009

Second Edition by Grimalhame Press 2012

Third Edition by Grimalhame Press 2025

Grimalhame
Press

This Book is Dedicated to

Those I've Known and Loved.

Together we danced paw in paw through flower meadows and sailed the stormy seas of troubled times. You are the earth on which I tread and the wind on which I soar.

Time

Spend Time on things that matter, don't waste it on things that don't.
Time is a precious commodity and once it has gone it cannot be replaced.
Use it wisely.

The World of Grimalkin

Grimalkins are very fond of stories and *"Dance of the Fire Cat"* is one of the oldest and best loved of all stories at Grimalhame. In times past, Grimalkins would sit by the communal fire and listen to the elders telling stories about how the world came to be, about the Great Mother Goddess and all Her good works, and regale them with tales about the great fire dragons of the South, the mystical unicorns of the North, the treasure-hoarding griffins of the East, and the wise old dragons of the sea in the West.

Such stories became the bedrock of Grimalkin society and bards, such as Eriffinn Aengus of the Golden Branch, were celebrated for their ability to remember all the stories passed down through the generations. Many a dark midwinter night has been spent listening to the tales of Old.

"Dance of the Fire Cat" is a creation myth whose origins are lost in the mists of time, a tale of how cats came into being according to cats. But all myths have a grain of truth about them, and who knows? Perhaps the celestial fire cat still walks among the cat-folk. Perhaps dragons do exist and maybe you will meet a unicorn the next time you visit the forest. Magic is very much alive and will appear to those who possess an open heart and open mind, and for those who know where to look.

Grimalhame Press

"Go back to the mortal world, Earth Child, and tell your kin about this place. Tell them that just because they cannot see us, we are not there. We are but a pawstep, a whisker, a thought away, and tell them to grieve no longer. Tell them of the place that waits for them when they leave the mortal world and we will be there to meet them on the threshold.

The Great Mother has made it so."

The Old Grimalkin Book of Thalaig

"There is loneliness in darkness, and in darkness a longing for the familiar, the safe and the known. In darkness there is nothing and nowhere. No light. No hope. No love.

Yet She created all things from the Great Nothingness, growing like tiny seeds that begin their long, silent journey upwards through the cloying blackness of the Earth.

I stood on the threshold of the night, looking with my weak, mortal eyes towards that which I could not see, but I could sense.

In darkness I stood, but then I saw you, and suddenly there was light."

Eriffinn Aengus of the Golden Branch,

Clowder Bard – 1103-1187

Introduction

It was a balmy summer evening, and the Great Arcadian Forest was lush and green and awash with wild, fragrant flowers nurtured by the light and warmth of the twin suns. Somewhere in the foliage a blackbird sung his song of joy to the dying day accompanied by the musical trilling of a tiny, solitary wren.

The light was beginning to fade and the hearth-fires had been lit in the deep caverns of Grimalhame in preparation for the evening's festivities. Cats busied themselves carrying flowers and garlands with which to decorate their tables, and musicians tuned their fiddles and pipes, the occasional jig or reel drifted playfully through the trees.

Midsummer, or *Adrach,* as it is known in Old Grimalkin, was a magical time for the Clowder of Grimalhame; the cats of Marishame, Orishame and the surrounding clowders all gathered together for a time of feasting, singing and dancing to celebrate the bounty of the forest and to give thanks to the Great Mother Goddess.

The youngsters of the clowder sat among the exposed roots of a gnarled, ancient beech tree at the feet of the clowder historian, and Deputy Clowder Mother, Imeldra Moonpaw. Her orange eyes twinkled enigmatically against her jet-black fur as she cast her gaze over the little gathering.

"Tell us a story!" they cried excitedly.

"Certainly," said Imeldra with a smile, "what kind of story would you like?"

"Tell us about the fire cat."

"Very well..."

The youngsters of Grimalhame fell silent and sat comfortably, waiting for Imeldra to begin.

"This is the story of how our brother-in-the-sky, the fire cat, was created. We, the first of the mortal creatures, are all born of the stars, and this is how we came to be:

"From the heart of a star he came, born from the chaos of creation. He came with the spark of divine light in his fiery paws and danced across the face of the sun at the beginning of the world. He danced far and wide, across the plains of Tharsis and the Great Harara Desert, planting the seeds of life in the barren ground in his wake. He sang his joyful song beneath the stars of the Great Divide:

"Awake my friends, for I am the first! Arise and join me in the dance of life. Be not sorrowful for there is no longer death and darkness."

And so, the first cats appeared from the womb of the sleeping earth to rejoice and sing in the First Days of the New Dawn.

Dance
of the
Fire Cat

In the beginning there was nothing. No time or space, no light or darkness. There was nothing except the Great Mother Goddess. Suddenly, a tiny pearl of light came into existence from the depths of Her soul. Inside this pearl were all of time and space and everything that was to come into being. It swelled and expanded, cooling down as it embarked on its never-ending odyssey.

And so was created the Great Divide.

Grimalhame Press

Grimalhame Press

The Great Mother Goddess was lonely in Her new creation. She longed for company, so She made the stars, the planets, and everything in between. She made the new world from a ball of ice and rock and shaped it until the first land features appeared. She kissed the small ball of ice and rock and, as She did, it became alight with magical fire.

The Great Mother Goddess shed tears for Her creation and those tears became the first oceans. She made the Day – a big, golden, male cat with a long, flowing mane, gilded fur and fluffy tail, who chased the daystars across the sky. His name was Shamash, which means *"Bright One'* in the ancient language.

Grimalhame Press

She made the Night; a female cat, dark as shadow, who curled around the world every evening, enveloping it in her soft velvet fur. Her name was Inghira, or *'Dark One'*. The stars that shone from her belly were the souls of those yet to be born.

Grimalhame Press

The Great Mother decided that Her new world should be home to all kinds of creatures. The Sphinx, the Phoenix, and the Chimera had already come into being, appearing instantaneously from the magical cosmic fires when the Universe was created, and facets of the Goddess Herself made real.

She reached inside the sun and pulled out a small orange cat. He lay curled up in the palm of Her hand, still as stone, and devoid of life. She placed a kiss on the small, striped head and he immediately awoke, stretched, yawned, and flexed his claws. Magical fire sprang from his head and licked playfully around his ears and sparks danced from his whiskers.

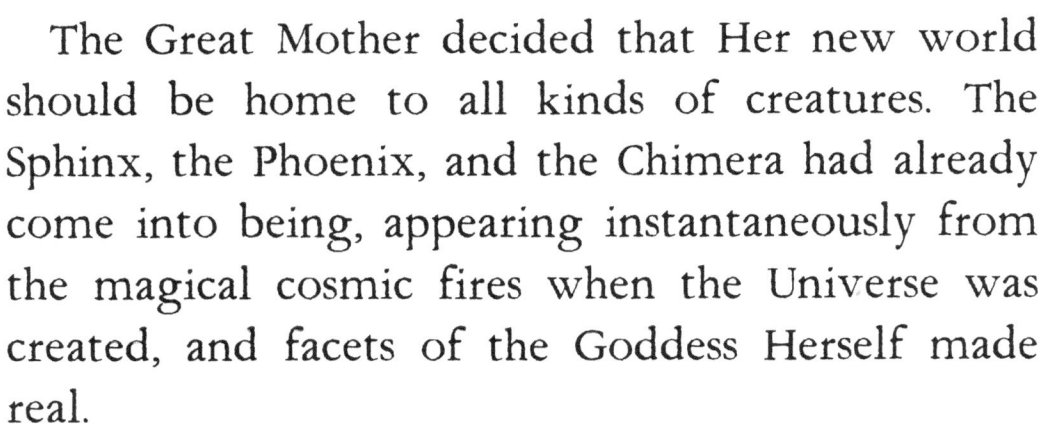

Fire danced from his back, paws and tail, sparkling and flickering in the darkness of the Great Divide. The Great Mother Goddess bestowed the gift of the Divine Spark inside the newly formed fire cat and set him down upon the earth. The little fire cat bounded away happily into the distance to begin his Dance of Life across the Far Dominions.

The fire cat felt so glad to be alive that he leapt in the air, twisting and somersaulting as he began his Dance of Life across the barren Plains of Amaris. He made vast leaps, spun, and hopped on his small orange legs, making circles and spirals in the dusty ground as he went. With each step the fire cat took he left behind a small seed of light in the ground like a tiny star that had fallen to earth - a *life-spark* - made real by the joy in his heart.

He stopped dead, crouched down on all fours, and stared wildly from side to side, his tail swishing this way and that like a fiery snake. Suddenly he raced off in the direction of the lurid glow in the distance with the trail of life-sparks glittering in his wake. His singing grew fainter as he made his way towards the horizon, and to Tharsis - the Land of the Fire Mountains.

On and on the little fire cat danced until he came to the border of the Sarpedon Flatlands. Before him lay an immense lake of liquid lava with sparks jumping from its surface. The fire cat knew he could not be harmed by fire, so he continued on his way across the fire-lake. Unfortunately, the fire-lake could not hold his weight, so he jumped, tip-toed and hop-skipped over the lava to prevent him from sinking. Islands of black basalt drifted sluggishly on the surface of the fire-lake, rocking lazily in the bubbling magma he leapt from island to island.

As he made his way across the fire-lake, he saw the great mountains of fire in the distance; huge, towering sentinels silhouetted against the red-orange sky, with fountains of magma belching into the air and cascading down their rugged sides. Lava oozed in long, slow-moving, glowing rivers making the landscape appear to be embraced in the coils of a world-serpent made from liquid fire. Hot geysers shot steaming vapours high into the sulfurous air showering the scorched earth with acidic fumes and spray. On he hurried, but his paws did not touch the lava long enough to leave behind a life-spark, and that is why, in the Beginning, there were no cats in Tharsis.

As the fire cat reached the borders of Tharsis, he found himself on the shores of the Ocean of Storms, the first ocean created by the Great Mother. The little fire cat paused, then sat down on the shoreline as the gentle waves lapped inches from his paws. He looked to the horizon with his keen orange eyes and saw a large island in the distance.

It looked so far away, and he wondered how he was ever going to get across the sea without a boat. The Great Mother heard his thoughts and took him in Her hand and lifted him into the sky. He felt the warm ocean wind support his body and at first, he was afraid. But as he looked down, he saw the beautiful deep blue-green colours of the ocean with the infinite Great Divide reflected on its surface.

Bright stars glinted and rippled with the motion of the water, making strange shapes as the lights merged, then moved apart. He saw ethereal star-cats leaping playfully after small fish that breached the surface of the ocean, and magnificent water-horses that galloped with wild abandon over the swell. He gazed down at the restless, heaving main beneath him; the rhythmic sound of the rolling ocean lulling him into a half-sleep as the Great Mother carried him gently across to the islands of the mid-ocean.

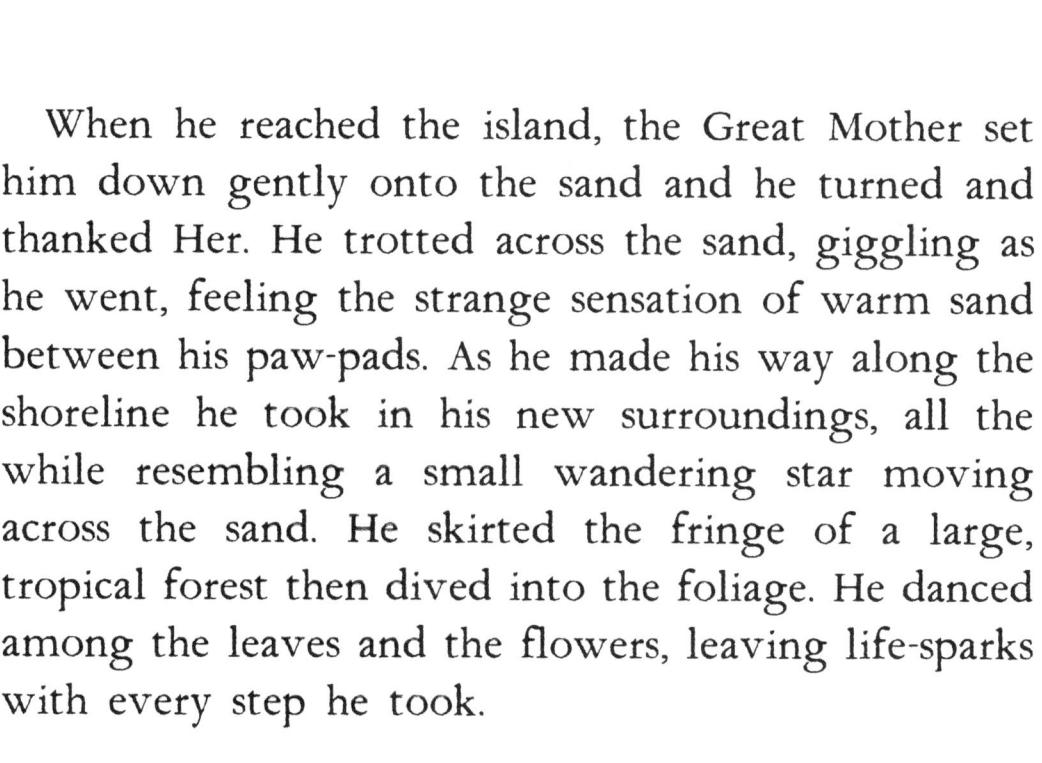

When he reached the island, the Great Mother set him down gently onto the sand and he turned and thanked Her. He trotted across the sand, giggling as he went, feeling the strange sensation of warm sand between his paw-pads. As he made his way along the shoreline he took in his new surroundings, all the while resembling a small wandering star moving across the sand. He skirted the fringe of a large, tropical forest then dived into the foliage. He danced among the leaves and the flowers, leaving life-sparks with every step he took.

The little fire cat breathed in deeply and smelled the exotic scents of the tropical paradise - the sharp, fruity smell of Sunburst orchid, and the cloying, spicy scents of strange nuts that hung in long bunches from the tops of the elegant, sloping palms that arched overhead. He was overcome with curiosity, and by the strange plants that surrounded him.

"The leaves are bigger than I am. Surely if I was to sit in one, I could sail across the ocean!" he pondered as he examined a particularly large frond.

Grimalhame Press

He stopped dancing every now and then to sniff at something here and taste something there. Inspired by the beautiful surroundings, he burst into song. He emerged from a dense clump of mangroves and found himself on the other side of the island. Once again, the wind currents caught the fire cat's small body and carried him back to the mainland, still singing as he was buffeted playfully by the clouds.

After being placed carefully down onto the earth once more by the Great Mother, he took stock of where he was. He stood on the threshold of the mighty Harara Desert and stared in wonderment at the vast expanse of undulating sand dunes. Golden hills stretched as far as the eye could see, the yellow of the dunes contrasting sharply with the bright, nebulous sky.

Grimalhame Press

The gas-giant planet of Aello hung as a gibbous crescent in the hot, hazy afternoon sky, its tiny shepherd moons reflecting the light from distant stars making them stand out against their gargantuan mother planet. Crystalline sand grains bounced down the dunes' shapely sides chased by the vagrant breeze, creating a low humming sound in the silence.

He leapt onto the sand and danced up and down the dunes, leaving bright life-sparks that glittered and shone in the sunlight where his fiery paws had touched the ground. The fire cat appeared like a miniature sun that rolled across the primordial landscape. As the fire cat danced, the trail of life-sparks made complex spiral patterns in the soft sand, turning this way and that, stretching the entire length of the Harara.

Grimalhame Press

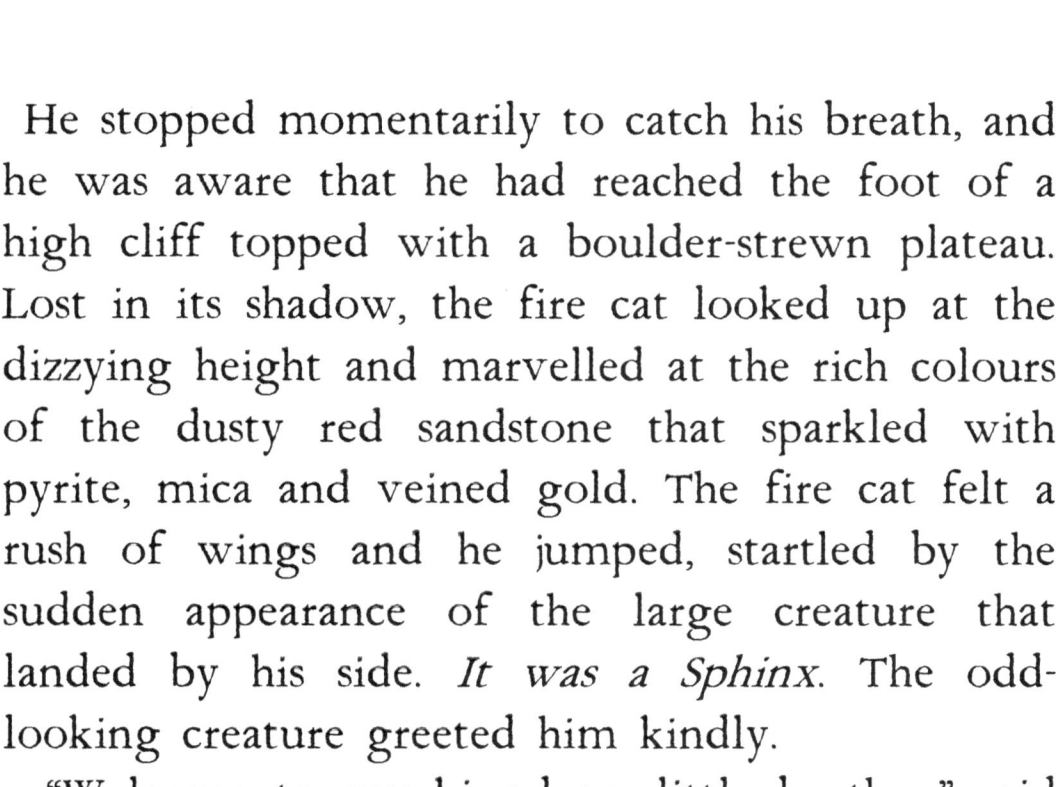

He stopped momentarily to catch his breath, and he was aware that he had reached the foot of a high cliff topped with a boulder-strewn plateau. Lost in its shadow, the fire cat looked up at the dizzying height and marvelled at the rich colours of the dusty red sandstone that sparkled with pyrite, mica and veined gold. The fire cat felt a rush of wings and he jumped, startled by the sudden appearance of the large creature that landed by his side. *It was a Sphinx.* The odd-looking creature greeted him kindly.

"Welcome to my kingdom, little brother," said the Sphinx, "I hope I find you well?"

The fire cat, awed by her size, felt very small indeed in her presence. She had rich, dark skin and her long, luxuriant hair blew freely in the desert wind, rippling like a sheet of liquid copper.

"Yes," he replied, "just a little tired."

The fire cat looked down at the ground averted his eyes from her steady gaze, feeling very small and insignificant. The Sphinx, sensing the fire cat's discomfort, spoke softly to him in a deep, musical voice like the chords of an ancient symphony, that seemed to touch his very heart.

"You are in Israfel; the Phoenix and I are the only creatures that dwell here. I trust the Great Mother has sent you to populate the world? I shall be glad of the company."

Suddenly, two life-sparks glowed brightly on the ground beneath the Sphinx's front paws. The ground opened up and, from underneath her right paw came a serval cat - yellow as sand - with black spots on her head, sides and haunches. She sported the most enormous ears the fire cat would ever see on a feline. The Sphinx touched the serval's forehead in blessing with her paw and it glowed momentarily with bright, unearthly light.

"You shall be my ears of the desert," said the Sphinx.

Again, the ground shuddered and from beneath the Sphinx's left paw emerged a red-pelted cat – the colour of desert stone - with the fierce light of battle in her green, gleaming eyes - a *caracal*. The Sphinx also put a forepaw to the caracal's head in blessing.

"You shall be my eyes of the desert,"

The Sphinx looked pleased as the two cats touched noses in greeting. The serval and the caracal were to be the first servants of the Sphinx who would be her eyes and ears in places where she could not see or hear, for they were blessed with supernatural hearing, sight and speed. This would be very important as the desert kingdom of Amaterasu would suffer great upheaval in the coming ages.

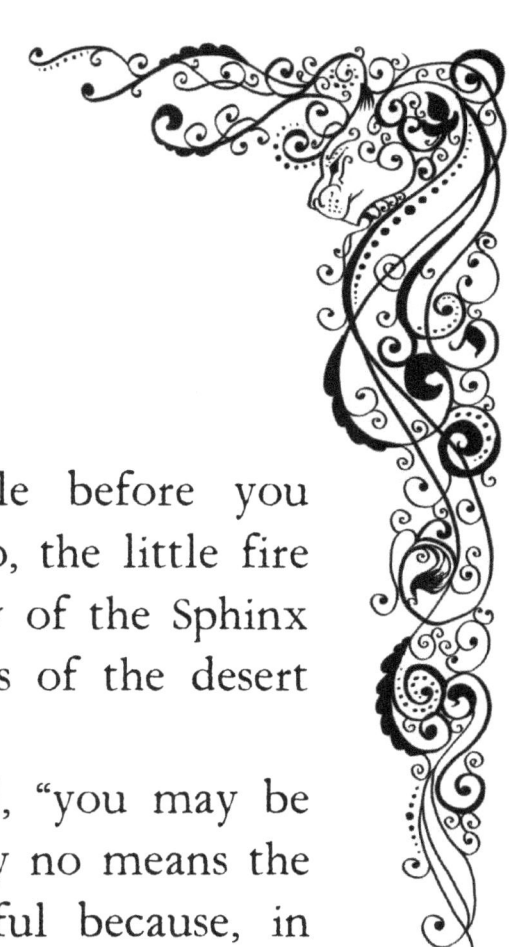

"Come, brother, and rest awhile before you continue on your way," she said. So, the little fire cat curled up beside the huge body of the Sphinx and she told him of all the secrets of the desert and the importance of his task.

"You see, little brother," she said, "you may be small, but this matters not. I am by no means the largest creature, but I am powerful because, in time, I will have to protect my creatures from the beings of the Dark Regions that could do great harm to the world."

The fire cat looked puzzled. He didn't like the sound of the beings of the Dark Regions at all. "But I have seen only beautiful things," he said, "how can this be?"

The Sphinx sighed. "It is the way of the Cosmos, little brother. We will not be alone in our existence. There will be other worlds far away, other galaxies, daystars, and other creatures. Sometimes, when beings live for a long time, they will forget where they came from and forget the Great Mother. They will become blinded by the material world and forget how to love. They will think only of themselves and mistreat their fellow creatures for their own gain or pleasure." There was sadness in her deep voice. "This will create an imbalance in the Cosmic Order."

"What is the Cosmic Order?" asked the fire cat, puzzled.

"The Cosmos must always stay in perfect balance and harmony; there must always be an equal amount of positive and negative forces in the Universe. Too many negative actions, such as creatures acting selfishly without any regard for their fellow beings, will create dangerous spirits that will be nourished by the suffering of innocent souls. These creatures will reside in the Lower Regions of existence and will have the ability to pass through into the mortal realm. As love and happiness die, so evil will be born and made real."

On seeing the fear on the little fire cat's face, she added:

"Do not worry, little brother, this has yet to be. The Phoenix, the Chimera and I have been sent as the first creatures of the Far Dominions to keep these lands safe from harm. There will be others who will join us in time, but that is far into the future. We are from another time, another Cosmos, and we come with great magic. You too have great magic; as you create with your love and joy, the magic is strengthened with every step you take. So you see, little brother, no matter how big or small you are you are an important part of the Cosmos. As long as you know how to love, you need never be afraid. Do you understand?"

The little fire cat, comforted by her words, looked up into her beautiful face and into her deep, amber eyes, and his heart swelled. Somehow, inside himself, he knew that this was so.

The fire cat and the Sphinx lay side by side and looked out over the desert kingdom to where the great city of Hamuk, the *City in the Sand,* would stand centuries from now, gazing in silence and contemplating what was to come.

After he was fully rested, the fire cat said goodbye to the Sphinx, the serval and the caracal, and went on his way. He danced through the vast green forests of Arcadia, and crossed golden meadows full of bright, scented flowers. He wandered through dense woodland that filtered the sunlight through the leaves, creating pools of watery light on the lush, green grass. He ventured beneath tumbling, rainbow-crested waterfalls and into cool, echoing, underground caves with the life-sparks shimmering behind him.

Grimalhame Press

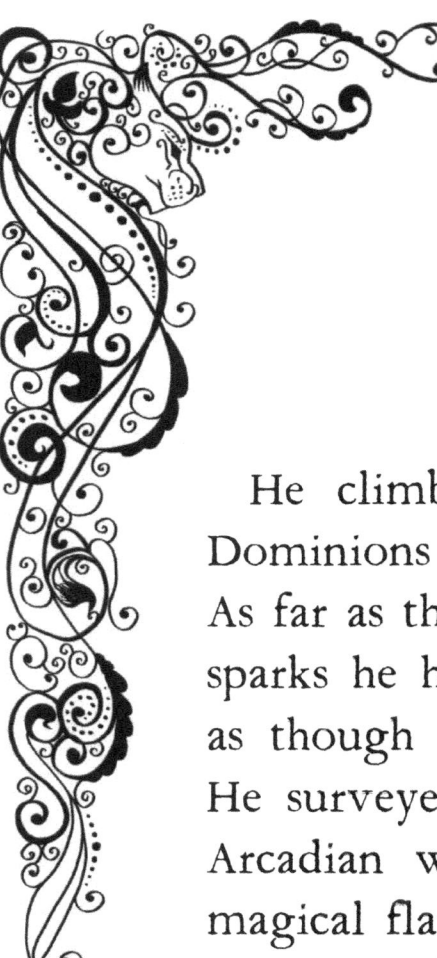

He climbed the highest mountain in the Far Dominions and looked down at the land below. As far as the eye could see were the glittering life-sparks he had left behind, illuminating the world as though the sky had been turned upside-down. He surveyed the scene with satisfaction, the keen Arcadian wind ruffling his fur and making the magical flames around his body flicker. In a voice that carried across every kingdom he called:

"Awake, my friends, for I am the first!
Arise and join me in the Dance of Life. Be not
sorrowful for there is no longer death and
darkness."

Grimalhame Press

One by one, the first cats emerged from the womb of the sleeping earth. They too, like the serval and caracal, stretched, yawned, and rubbed their sleepy eyes. They looked around and saw many others of their kind; ounce, wildcat, lynx, forest cat, puma, tiger, leopard, ocelot, cheetah, sabretooth and lion; so many varieties and in every shape, size and colour.

Grimalhame Press

"*A cat for every kingdom,*" he thought as he watched the new cats touch noses and greet each other with head rubbing and the intermingling of whiskers.

The little fire cat felt very happy as he saw all the cats of the Far Dominions together under the twin suns; this would be the only time they would be united for, after his departure, they would go their separate ways to start their new lives and have families of their own.

Grimalhame Press

The fire cat leapt from his high precipice and bounded down the mountain to join them. He ran pell-mell through the Great World Forest and was greeted by many cats who danced and ran with him through the trees. He came to a clearing surrounded by three rings of colossal standing stones on which were carved strange and mysterious runes and symbols – *the language of the Cosmos*. He turned to the cats who had followed him through the forest and said:

"This is where you shall gather at every full moon to sing and dance beneath the stars. The whole forest belongs to you - it shall be called *Grimalhame – 'cat-home"*

The new forest cats cheered and hurried off in different directions to explore their new surroundings. Many formed a circle in the middle of the Henge and sang and joined paws in feline unity. They danced together in the clearing while the fire cat joined them, hopping on tiptoe in and out of the throng.

Grimalhame Press

But something strange was happening, something the forest cats had not expected - *the suns were setting*. Suddenly, the dancing stopped, and the cats fell silent. Apprehension and confusion hung over the gathering as the suns disappeared further below the skyline. The sky grew darker, and the cats cowered down in fear - they knew nothing of the night or of darkness. They looked to the fire cat with wide, frightened eyes.

"We are afraid, O fire cat, what of the sunshine?" they cried.

"Here the suns end their daily rule," he called, "fear not the Dark One for she brings rest to the weary soul."

Reassured by the fire cat's words, they joined paws and formed a dancing circle. Round and round the Henge they danced, paw in paw, as the suns faded into twilight and the moons appeared over the horizon. The cats of the forest sang and laughed in the half-light for they were no longer afraid. The coming of Inghira, the Dark One, was indeed a blessing. As the last ray of sunlight died and the Dark One curled around the world, enveloping it in her deep, velvet pelt, magical portals opened up around them; bright shining doors to the world of the spirits who would bring great magic and wisdom into their lives.

Out came the nature spirits, the faeys and the elementals, and they danced and sang with the cats in their revelry. And so, the cats of the forest spent their first night beneath the wide, starry sky.

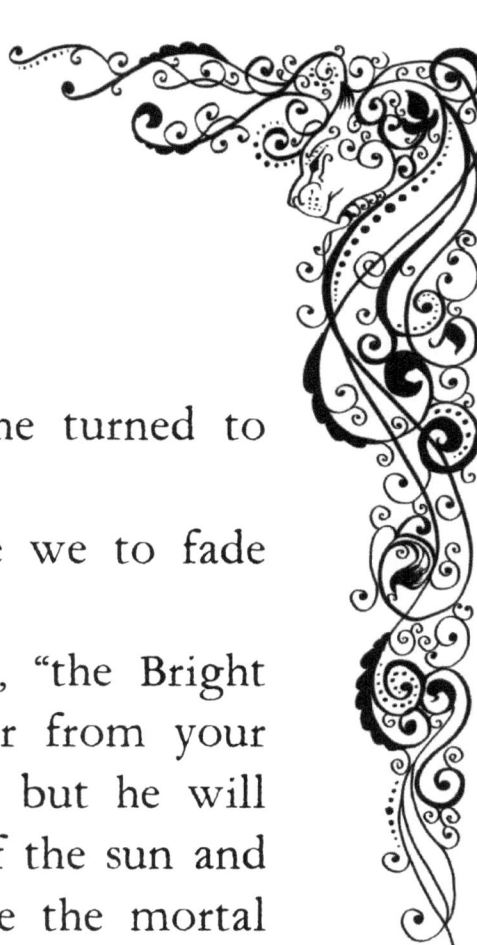

The fire cat's work was done. As he turned to leave, a voice behind him spoke:

"But what will become of us? Are we to fade and die like the Bright One?"

"No, my friends," said the fire cat, "the Bright One does not die. He may disappear from your sight as his mate rules the darkness, but he will reappear again at dawn. I am born of the sun and I, in turn, made you. You will leave the mortal world one day, but you shall never truly die. This I promise."

And with this knowledge, cats – *Grimalkins* – everywhere watched the Bright One's progress across the sky, disappear at night and then rise again the following day. They knew that after their mortal bodies were spent, their spirits would return to dance joyously across the earth once more.

The fire cat stood alone in the forest. He looked tired and sad. He lay down in the grass and sighed. He was so exhausted he could barely keep his eyes open. He could feel his magical fire beginning to fail. The forest cats gathered around him, whispering to one another in anxious voices.

The Great Mother Goddess reached down and took the weary little fire cat in Her arms and lifted him into the sky. He took one last look at the singing and dancing cats below enjoying their new lives with each other, and he smiled.

The Great Mother smiled too, for She was very proud of Her little fire cat. All over the new world, cats everywhere looked up and saw him being borne away by the Great Mother back to the Great Divide; the fire cat's light still visible, reflected in their shining eyes as he ascended. All cats gazed as one; from the mighty tiger in his oceanic paradise to the sabretooth in his stronghold of the desert kingdom, and to the small and humble forest cat in her new-found home of Grimalhame. The Sphinx, flanked by her servants, also turned skyward for she too was very proud.

Grimalhame Press

He got to his feet in the palm of the Great Mother's hand and leapt back into the heart of the red sun and it became hot. It became so hot that it swelled to twice its size and turned bright yellow. It radiated a myriad of glittering stars in a single blast, sending stellar dust and light outward in a million different directions. The magical flames of the fire cat had made the red sun twice as bright as it was before. The fire cat's task now was to keep Shamash company: while Shamash rolled the big sun across the sky during the day, so the fire cat rolled the smaller, second sun around Shamash.

To this day, the cats of the Far Dominions can look up and see the face of the fire cat in the sky, his rays of magical fire cascading from his bright orange fur and the sparks dancing from his whiskers. Every now and then, he comes down from the Great Divide to sing and dance with the children of the first cats he brought into the world. Every summer solstice, the Grimalkins of the Clowder of Grimalhame re-enact the Dance of the Fire Cat to give thanks to him and the Great Mother Goddess for their being.

The Ocean Lord

Book Two of the Fire Cat Stories

"The fire cat looked towards the entrance of the cave on the opposite side of the lagoon and waited and, for a moment, he saw nothing. Then a large bow wave slowly appeared from the cave. It travelled towards him, and the fire cat held his breath in anticipation, his heart pounding. The bow wave grew bigger, rippling as it came nearer.

It stopped short of the rock ledge he was sitting on, and then the water suddenly went still. Seconds ticked by as the fire cat peered into the clear, turquoise water. It was deathly silent. Suddenly, the water boiled and frothed as a huge something emerged from the water, sending waves crashing over the ledge. The fire cat was taken totally by surprise and rolled over onto his side, seawater splashing over him.

A dark shadow cast itself over the fire cat's prone form as the massive creature rose slowly from the depths of the lagoon. The fire cat's strength left him as he lay in the shadow of the creature that fixed him with an unearthly gaze that rooted him helplessly to the spot."

The Ocean Lord is the second of the Fire Cat stories and follows the fire cat from his home in the Great Divide to the ancient and magical Clowder of Grimalhame.

After meeting Winnowyn and Rowanberry Longwhisker, the Clowder Elders, the fire cat sets out on a mission to find a cure for the mysterious illness that is afflicting the Clowder and the creatures of the Great Arcadian Forest. His journey takes him beyond the shores of Arcadia to Kaldivari, the kingdom of the Tiger Lords, and to Tharsis, the Land of the Fire Mountains.

With the Clowder in grave danger, the fire cat must face his greatest fear and go beyond the boundary of death itself in order to save his kin.

Can he find the Ocean Lord, the Source of All Wisdom, before it is too late?

About the Author

Angela Russell lives in South Shields, Tyneside, and has several poems and short stories published in anthologies through United Press London including *Angel's Breath, Poetry By Moonlight, Fact and Fantasy, Portraits in Pen, Whispers on the Breeze, The Funny Thing, Reflections, A Message to You, Poets of the Year 2008 and 2009, and Poetry Diary 2009 and 2010.*

Angela achieved the accolade of Best in Category for Writer of the Year 2011, also through United Press London. She has also had both poetry and artwork published in the limited edition *Moonwise Diary 2010* by William Morris.
An illustrator by trade, Angela has also exhibited work in the Great North Museum Hancock, and the Tate Modern London.

As a member of the Order of Bards, Ovates and Druids, Angela continues to write and illustrate children's books, drawing on aspects of mythology, magic, world culture, history, and her native Scots-Irish, Romany, and Geordie roots.

Grimalhamepress.co.uk
Grimalhame Press®
Clowder of Grimalhame®

Author's Notes

AI

AI should never be used as a crutch or a replacement for real-world art. I am an illustrator so understand the importance of developing real-world skills and supporting other creators. AI can fill gaps in knowledge, offer another perspective or dimension, create a spark of inspiration, worldbuilding, concepts, and provide one with images of things and places that are otherwise inaccessible. It is a tool and should be treated as such.

I respect the views and opinions of other creators regarding AI; I too can see the dangers and risks regarding it, which is why it should be used responsibly.

So, I will say this – *use AI responsibly*. Support real-world artists, musicians, writers and creators. Buy their work. Promote their work online. Host their work in galleries. It's very important that we keep old skills alive. Use AI if you choose, but keep it in its place, because it can so easily get out of control, or be abused in ways it was never meant for.

"I would hate to know everything,
for there would be no joy in discovery."

Rowanberry Evander Longwhisker

Strength, Courage, Fortitude

Longwhisker Family Motto

"East or West,
'Hame's Best"

www.ingramcontent.com/pod-product-compliance
Lightning Source LLC
Chambersburg PA
CBHW040610260626
47164CB00022BA/206